PLEASE, KEEP WARM.

FOR MOM.

SORRY ABOUT THE BAD WORDS.

"THIS MUST BE THE PLACE"
A PLEASE KEEP WARM COLLECTION BY MICHAEL SWEATER.

PUBLISHED BY SILVER SPROCKET.
FIRST PRINTING, SUMMER 2017.
PRINTED IN CANADA.

SILVER SPROCKET CATALOG NUMBER 77.
ISBN 978-1-945509-14-8

PLEASE KEEP WARM!
FUGAZI

UNCLE STAN?
YES CLOVER?

FUGAZI
WHAT DO YOU THINK IS BETTER?
DINOSAURS OR WITCHES?

I DON'T KNOW.
I THINK DINOSAURS HAVE COOL TEETH.

I GUESS DINOSAURS ARE OKAY.

CAN YOU PLAY QUIETLY FOR A LITTLE BIT?
I REALLY NEED TO FOCUS ON FINDING IDEAS FOR MY NOVEL.
I HAVE AN IDEA FOR A NOVEL.

IT'S ABOUT A BEAUTIFUL PRINCESS NAMED CLOVER!

ALSO, THERE IS A DINOSAUR BECAUSE THEY HAVE COOL TEETH.

HEY, CATMAN?
CAN YOU WATCH CLOVER FOR A LITTLE BIT SO I CAN WORK ON MY NOVEL?

PLEASE?
JUST FOR AN HOUR.

THIS ISN'T A GOOD TIME STAN.
I'M TRYING TO FIGURE OUT HOW TO PAY A 900-DOLLAR BILL WITH 720 DOLLARS.

PRETTY PLEASE?

CAN YOU PLAY QUIETLY WHILE I DO THIS?

WHAT DO YOU THINK IS BETTER?
DINOSAURS OR WITCHES?

THIS IS MY FAVORITE EPISODE OF WIZARD WARS.
BELZOR THINKS HE IS STRONG, BUT HE ISN'T THAT STRONG.
FIRE MAGIC IS SO STUPID!

HEY GUYS! WHAT ARE WE WATCHING?

FLOWER!
IT'S SO GOOD TO SEE YOU!

CAN YOU WATCH CLOVER FOR A MINUTE?
THANK YOU SO MUCH, BYE!

IF I WAS A WIZARD, I'D PROBABLY BE SOMETHING COOL. LIKE A NECROMANCER.

I THINK DOING YOGA COULD BE A REAL FORCE FOR POSITIVE CHANGE IN YOUR LIFE.
ALSO, THE FRESH AIR WOULD DO YOU GOOD.
I ALREADY KNOW HOW TO DO A YOGA!
TOE TOUCHIES!
THE PUPPY!
COBRA SNAKE!

HEY GUYS.
CAN WE KEEP IT DOWN A LITTLE BIT?

OH!
HEY STAN!

CAN YOU WATCH CLOVER FOR A LITTLE WHILE?
END!

HEY STAN? CAN YOU GIVE MY BLACK METAL DEMO A LISTEN?
OF COURSE!

I THINK THE FILE IS MESSED UP.
IT SOUNDS LIKE STATIC AND A PERSON RATTLING A BAG OF OLD SODA CANS.

PERFECT!
NOW I JUST HAVE TO RECORD THE VOCALS!

THE MOON LIGHT TEARS THROUGH YOUR HEART,
THE FATED MOMENT APPROACHES!

FEELING YOUR BONES DEPART,
AS YOU STEP INTO THE WARLOCK CIRCLE!

SORRY FOR INTERRUPTING!
DID YOU WANT A BOWL OF CEREAL?

WITH SUGAR PLEASE!

STANLEY! CATMAN! I DID IT!
MY DEMO IS FINALLY FINISHED! IT'S EVEN GOT A HIDDEN TRACK SONG ABOUT A WIZARD!

THAT'S AWESOME CLOVER!
WHEN DOES IT RELEASE?

WHAT DO YOU MEAN "RELEASE?"
I ALREADY FINISHED IT.
IT'S RIGHT HERE!

THAT'S JUST PART ONE! NOW YOU GOTTA SET UP DISTRIBUTION, SEND OUT PRESS RELEASES, SET UP YOUR SOCIAL MEDIAS.
AN ALBUM IS A MULTI-YEAR-LONG COMMITMENT!

WHAT THE HECK!
I KNEW I SHOULD HAVE JUST MADE A MOVIE ABOUT SPACESHIPS!

SO THIS IS IT!
MY STANDARD BOILER PLATE MUSIC MANAGEMENT CONTRACT.

FOR HALF OWNERSHIP AND 50 PERCENT OF THE PROFITS I WILL DEAL WITH BOOKING, DISTRIBUTION, MERCH, AND ALL THAT SORT OF STUFF ARTISTS LIKE YOU HATE.

THIS IS ALL STUFF I CAN DO BY MYSELF ALREADY!
WHY DO YOU GET HALF OF EVERYTHING I MAKE FOR THAT?!

BECAUSE I WILL ACTUALLY DO IT.

I WONDER WHAT THE INTERNET THINKS ABOUT ALL OF MY NEW SONGS.
I BET THE ONE ABOUT THE SKELETONS IS REAL POPULAR!

WHERE IS THE BUTTON THAT MAKES PEOPLE LIKE MY ART?

WHAT'S BOTHERING MY LITTLE CLOVER? SADNESS IS A NEW LOOK FOR YOU!
LEAVE ME ALONE.

DON'T BE MEAN! I JUST WANTED TO KNOW WHAT IS UP.

MY BLACK METAL DEMO IS AWFUL AND EVERYONE ON THE INTERNET THINKS I AM A POSER.
ALSO WE ARE OUT OF MILK.

WHY IS CLOVER CRYING IN THE HALLWAY?

HER ALBUM WAS REVIEWED BY PITCHFORK.
I'M SO SORRY.

THEY GAVE IT FIVE STARS!

WATCHING CLOVER WORKING ON MUSIC HAS GOT ME EXCITED TO FINALLY WORK ON MY NOVEL.

HASN'T SHE BEEN A DEPRESSED MESS ALL WEEK?

YEAH.
IT'S SO ROMANTIC.

LITTLE CLOVER! WHY HAVE YOU BEEN LAYIN' IN BED ALL DAY?
IS THERE ANYTHING YOU NEED TO TALK ABOUT? I'M A REAL GOOD LISTENER!

YOU ALWAYS KNOW EXACTLY WHAT TO DO ALL THE TIME.
YOU WOULDN'T EVEN KNOW HOW TO UNDERSTAND.

WHAT WOULD A GUY LIKE YOU EVEN KNOW ABOUT BEING SAD?!

I HAPPEN TO KNOW A THING OR TWO ABOUT DEPRESSION.

I WAS GOTH IN HIGH SCHOOL!

HEY CHUBSTER! DON'T YOU WRITE FOR THE SCHOOL PAPER?

WHY ARE YOU DRESSING LIKE A COLOR BLIND DUBSTEP ENTHUSIAST?

I'VE BEEN MEANING TO ASK THE SAME THING. PEOPLE HAVE BEEN LOOKING AT US A LOT.

OH, I'M GOTH JUST LIKE YOU NOW!

I'VE BEEN REALLY FEELING THE DARKNESS IN THE LITTLE MOMENTS.
GETTING INTO THE CURE PRETTY HARD.

YEAH. I'M PRETTY MUCH A NIHILIST NOW.

HOW ARE WE GOING TO FINISH BY THREE? WE WASTED TOO MUCH TIME PLAYING WITH FONTS AGAIN!
LET'S JUST COPY SOMETHING FROM THE REAL PAPER. THIS IRAQ THING SEEMS PRETTY COOL.

YOU CAN'T JUST COPY THE ARTICLE! THAT'S PLAGIARISM!

IF COPYING IS WRONG YOU NEED TO GIVE DILBERT A CALL AND APOLOGIZE FOR THAT NERDY SHIRT.

YOU ARE ONE TO TALK ABOUT ANYONE ELSE'S FASHION CHOICES AFTER PAYING FOR THOSE PANTS.
WHY ARE THEY SO LARGE?

NUMBER ONE, MY DAD PAID FOR THEM.

ALSO, I LIKE THE EXTRA LEG ROOM. IT'S LIKE FLYING FIRST CLASS, BUT FOR PANTS.

AND THAT'S ABOUT IT.
EVERYTHING THIS OL' CAT KNOWS ABOUT BEING GOTH.

DO YOU UNDERSTAND WHAT I'M TRYING TO TELL YOU?

THAT IF I WANT TO KNOW TRUE DESPAIR, I NEED TO GET BIGGER PANTS?

OH LITTLE CLOVER. BEING GOTH ISN'T ABOUT THE SIZE OF YOUR PANTS.

BEING GOTH IS ABOUT THE SIZE OF YOUR HEART.

SHOW ME SHOW ME SHOW ME HOW TO DO THAT TRICK...

I'M A FRAUD.
I'LL NEVER BE ABLE TO WRITE AN AUTHENTIC BLACK METAL ALBUM.

I AM A TITAN OF MISERY.

IF I AIM FOR FUNERAL DOOM, MAYBE I CAN FAIL INTO A 90S EMO THING...

CATMAN! ARE YOU EATING GRASS? IS IT BECAUSE YOU FEEL SICK?

I READ ON WIKIPEDIA THAT CATS DO THAT WHEN THEY GET SICK.

SINCE YOUR OLD BAND BROKE UP I'VE BEEN TRYING TO FIND WAYS TO CUT BACK ON MY EXPENSES.
I'VE BEEN EATING DANDELIONS FOR LUNCH ALL WEEK.

IF YOU DON'T HAVE MUCH MONEY YOU CAN ALWAYS EAT RAMEN!

I LIKE TO PUT AN EGG AND LITTLE PIECES OF CHICKEN IN IT!

IF I COULD BUY EGGS I WOULDN'T BE SITTING IN THE YARD EATING GRASS.
ALSO, I CAN'T AFFORD WATER.

HOW CAN YOU DRINK COFFEE EVERY MORNING? IT'S SO STINKY.
WHAT? IT'S NOT STINKY, IT'S BOLD!

IT'S A REINVIGORATING AND HEARTY BREW. THE PERFECT WAY TO KICK START YOUR DAY.

NO WAY.
IT DOESN'T EVEN HAVE MARSHMALLOWS.

STAN! OUR HOUSEMATE CONTRACT SPECIFICALLY FORBIDS USING THE WRONG DISHES IN AN ATTEMPT TO AVOID WASHING THE ONES YOU NEED!

HOW DARE YOU THROW AROUND ACCUSATIONS!
YOU HAVE MASSIVELY MISJUDGED WHAT IS HAPPENING HERE!

I LIKE MY CEREAL REAL FLAT.

ALRIGHT STAN! TODAY IS THE DAY!
LET'S DO THIS THING.

I HAVE THE WHOLE DAY SET ASIDE TO START WORKING ON MY NOVEL.

I HAVE THE HOUSE ALL TO MYSELF!

THE INTERNET WAS SHUT OFF BECAUSE WE DIDN'T PAY THE BILL AGAIN!

I HAVE ALL THE TIME I COULD WANT AND NO DISTRACTIONS.

I FEEL SO PATHETIC.
I DON'T KNOW WHY I JUST CAN'T GET MYSELF TO WORK ON ANYTHING.

I ALWAYS FEEL THIS WAY RIGHT BEFORE I DO A THING I AM REALLY PROUD OF.

OH.
I SHOULD PROBABLY GET UP AND TAKE A SHOWER.

WEREN'T YOU TAKING THE DAY OFF TO WORK ON YOUR NOVEL?
I AM WORKING. IT'S CALLED RESEARCH.

I THOUGHT YOUR BOOK WAS ABOUT TEENAGE APATHY AND THAT KINDA STUFF.
WHY ARE YOU WATCHING DIE HARD ON CABLE?

BECAUSE WE DON'T HAVE IT ON DVD.

GUYS! YOU KNOW HOW I HAVE BEEN TRYING TO DECIDE WHAT TO WRITE MY BOOK ABOUT?
YEAH.

I THINK I HAVE A REALLY GOOD STARTING POINT!
YEAH?

CATCHER IN THE RYE MEETS DIE HARD!

OK STAN, JUST WRITE WHAT YOU KNOW.
"CHESTER LOOKED DOWN AT HIS FEET. HE KNEW THAT THE FUTURE WOULD BE EVERY BIT AS HORRIBLE AS HE IMAGINED IT COULD BE..."

...
SHOOT! I'M STUCK AGAIN.

OH YEAH.
"BUT ON THE BRIGHT SIDE, HE KNEW DEEP IN HIS HEART THAT POP PUNK WOULD NEVER DIE."

HEY GUYS.
I'VE BEEN THINKING A LOT LATELY AND MAYBE WE GOTTA DO SOMETHING ABOUT THIS CAPITALISM THING.

LIKE, YOU GUYS KNOW I'M NOT INTO POLITICS OR ANYTHING,
BUT I'VE BEEN WATCHING THIS BERNIE GUY ON THE YOUTUBE AND I AM GETTING ALL RILED UP.

OH MAN, I GOTTA SIT DOWN.
WHAT ARE WE WATCHING?

GAME OF THRONES.

SWEET.

HEY CLOVER, DO YOU MIND DOING AN INTERVIEW WITH A LOCAL ZINE?
WHY?

BECAUSE WE HAVE TO PROMOTE YOUR ALBUM SO WE CAN SELL ALBUMS AND ADD VEGETABLES TO OUR DIET AGAIN.
WHY?

BECAUSE I AM GOING TO NEED A LOT OF ENERGY IF YOU'RE GOING TO GO THROUGH THIS PHASE.
WHY?

LET'S TRY TO GET THROUGH THIS INTERVIEW QUICK. I HAVE AN APPOINTMENT WITH A SIX PACK AND A BLANKET IN AN HOUR.

IT'S IMPORTANT TO BE ON TIME FOR THINGS.

OKAY, DO YOU HAVE ANY ADVICE FOR OTHER YOUNG PEOPLE LOOKING TO BREAK INTO THE BLACK METAL SCENE?

IF YOU CAN'T BALANCE ON A SKATEBOARD, THAT'S OKAY.
IF YOU WANT YOU CAN JUST SIT ON IT AND ROLL DOWN HILLS!

I DON'T KNOW!
YOUR EARS MAKE ME NERVOUS.

THIS IS MY LIZARD, NEWTON!

HE LIKES GRAPES, AND HIS PLASTIC LOG, AND LYING IN THE SUN!

WHY ARE YOU TELLING ME THIS?
BECAUSE, NEWTON THINKS YOU'RE CUTE!

YOU ARE GOING TO LOVE OUTSIDE LITTLE NEWTON.
I WILL SHOW YOU MY FAVORITE TREE!

THE LEAVES LOOK SO BEAUTIFUL!
JUST WAIT UNTIL YOU GET TO SEE THEM IN THE FALL.

IT'S VERY IMPORTANT TO SPEND TIME IN NATURE!

CLOVER, WHY ARE YOU SLEEPING IN THE YARD?
WHERE IS YOUR LITTLE LIZARD GUY?

I WAS SHOWING NEWTON THE TREE AND THEN WE FELL ASLEEP.

OH NO! WHERE IS LITTLE NEWTON?!

CALM DOWN, IF YOU WERE A LIZARD, WHERE WOULD YOU BE?

DON'T WORRY CLOVER.
WE'RE GOING TO FIND YOUR LITTLE LIZARD BUDDY.

HE COULDN'T HAVE GOTTEN TOO FAR.
UNLESS LIZARDS ARE FAST.
ARE LIZARDS FAST GUYS?

WHAT DO YOU KNOW ABOUT LIZARDS?
HIS NAME IS NEWTON.

STAY OFF OF THAT.
THOSE ARE IMPORTANT DOCUMENTS. WE NEED THOSE.

STOP TOUCHING MY STUFF NEWTON.
I AM VERY BUSY.

WILL WHOEVER IS RESPONSIBLE FOR THIS LIZARD PLEASE COME SCOOP HIM?

YOU ARE MY BEST FRIEND.

YOU HAVE THE CUTEST LITTLE FEET!

I SHOULD ALSO GET A CAT.

MR. FLOWER,
YOU LOOK BORED!

HEY CATMAN, HOW ARE THOSE BILLS COMING ALONG?

OKAY I GUESS.
JUST TRYING TO MAKE THE NUMBERS WORK.

HOW BAD IS IT?

YOU KNOW THE END OF JURASSIC PARK?
WHERE THE RAPTORS ARE CLOSING IN, AND AT THE LAST MINUTE THE T-REX BREAKS IN AND EATS THE CRAP OUT OF THE RAPTORS?

YEAH.

I DON'T THINK THE T-REX IS COMING.

HEY STAN, CAN I HELP YOU WITH THE DISHES?
I'LL DO A PRETTY GOOD JOB.
SURE YOU CAN CLOVER. DO YOU WANT TO RINSE?

NO.
THAT'S FINE!
DO YOU WANT TO WASH?

I DON'T WANT TO DO THAT EITHER.

THOSE ARE PRETTY MUCH THE ONLY TWO PARTS OF WASHING DISHES.

OH.
I'M GOING TO GO WATCH THE TV.

WHY ARE WE LOOKING AT RECORDS?
DIDN'T I JUST LOAN YOU A DOLLAR FOR COFFEE?
MUDBUG!

THERE IS A SACRED SPACE AT THE CENTER OF THIS PLACE FOR THE RICH AND BROKE ALIKE.

THE FREE PILE!

A ZINE ABOUT EATING OUT OF THE TRASH AND A BLUEGRASS THRASH DEMO?
WHO IS THE TARGET AUDIENCE FOR THIS KIND OF STUFF?

YOU'RE THINKING ABOUT IT ALL WRONG DUDE.
SOMETIMES ART CAN BE ABOUT SOMEONE'S PERSONAL EXPRESSION OR EXPERIENCES.
SOME THINGS ARE ABOUT MORE THAN JUST SALES, CATMAN.

OH, I GET IT. IT'S LIKE ARTSCHOOL!
WHAT KIND OF CUTTING-EDGE PIECE OF WORK ARE YOU READING?

A THIRD EYE BLIND FANZINE.

IT'S HARD TO BELIEVE A ZINE COULD BE SO WELL-WRITTEN.
ANIME RULES

HAVE YOU EVER READ SOMETHING AND FELT YOUR LIFE CHANGING?

YEAH.
I LOVED GOOSEBUMPS!

HEY STAN,
WHAT ARE YOU READING?

I FOUND THIS ZINE ON THE FREE TABLE AT THE RECORD STORE AND I HAVEN'T BEEN ABLE TO PUT IT DOWN.

IT'S AN AMAZING PIECE OF WORK THAT TRANSCENDS THE MEDIUM.
YOU HAVE TO READ IT WHEN YOU GET A CHANCE!

I HAVE READ IT.
THAT'S MY ZINE. I MADE IT.

YOU MADE THIS?!

MY NAME IS ON THE COVER.
OH.

YOUR ZINE IS ONE OF THE MOST WELL-WRITTEN THING I HAVE EVER READ.

I REALLY THINK YOU SHOULD TRY YOUR HAND AT WRITING SOMETHING MORE SERIOUS.
HAVE YOU EVER THOUGHT ABOUT WRITING A NOVEL?

I DON'T EVEN KNOW WHAT I WOULD WRITE ABOUT ANYWAY.

THAT'S THE BEAUTY OF IT!
YOU CAN WRITE ABOUT ANYTHING YOU WANT!

I WONDER IF ANYONE HAS WRITTEN A NOVEL ABOUT SPACE...

HEY FLOWER, WHY DO YOU LOOK STRESSED OUT TODAY?

TRYING TO THINK OF AN IDEA FOR A NOVEL.

I HAD NO IDEA YOU WANTED TO WRITE A NOVEL!

WHAT?
NO.

I JUST NEED A QUICK WAY TO MAKE SOME MONEY.

HOW DOES ANYONE EVER KNOW WHAT TO WRITE A NOVEL ABOUT?

OH YEAH!
WIZARDS!

HEY, FLOWER. WHY ARE YOU ASLEEP OUT HERE?
I WAS WRITING ALL NIGHT.

CAN YOU TAKE A LOOK AT MY FIRST CHAPTER?

IS THIS JUST HARRY POTTER IN SPACE?
NO. I CHANGED THE NAMES!

I DID IT!

YOU LOOK BORED.
DO YOU WANT TO GO OUTSIDE AND DO SOMETHING?

SURE, WHAT DO YOU WANNA DO?

I DON'T THINK I REMEMBER WHAT PEOPLE DO OUTSIDE.

WHY IS STAN LAUGHING?
HE HAS BEEN MAKING THE PRANK CALLS ALL MORNING.

OH! CAN I TRY ONE?!
SURE! HAVE A SHOT!

HELLO! IS THIS THE COPS?
I SAW A WEREWOLF!
CLOVER NO!!!

HEY FLOWER, CAN I TELL YOU A SECRET?

SURE! AS LONG AS IT'S NOT WEIRD.

I DON'T REALLY LIKE MINOR THREAT OR FUGAZI.

OH MAN! ME EITHER! CAN I TELL YOU A SECRET TOO?!

YEAH!
I DON'T LIKE BLACK FLAG!

I DON'T LIKE THIS GAME ANYMORE...

I USED TO PLAY CHECKERS WITH MY GRANDMA EVERY WEEKEND.

SHE WOULD ALWAYS TELL ME THE SAME STORIES OVER AND OVER EVERY TIME.

HER STORIES WERE SO LONG I WOULD START TO FALL ASLEEP FROM THE BOREDOM.

SOMETIMES I WOULD WANT TO JUST GET UP AND LEAVE!

CLOVER?

YOUR GRAFFITI IS ALWAYS TOO POLITICAL.
WHAT?

WHY DON'T YOU DO SOMETHING COOL OR ARTISTIC?
LIKE A SKULL OR SOMETHING.

IF YOU DON'T STAND UP FOR WHAT YOU BELIEVE IN, YOU WILL END UP ALONE AND COMPLETELY IGNORED.

WELL CAN YOU WRITE SOMETHING FOR ME?

ANIME RULES

MAN, I'VE BEEN THINKING ABOUT GOING BACK TO COMMUNITY COLLEGE.

HAVE YOU LOST YOUR MIND?

COLLEGE IS THE BIGGEST SCAM IN THE BOOK!

I KNOW MAN, BUT WHAT AM I GONNA DO WHEN MY GIRLFRIEND FINALLY KICKS ME TO THE CURB?

I GUESS I JUST KINDA FIGURED YOU WOULD COME TO THE PARK AND LIVE IN A TREE WITH ME OR SOMETHING.

BEST FRIENDS!

EW!
WHY DO YOU HAVE A CAT?!

JAMES?
HE IS A LITTLE ANGEL!

DO YOU KNOW HOW MANY BIRDS THE AVERAGE CAT KILLS? JAMES IS A LITTLE MONSTER!

YES.

YOU THINK YOU'RE SO TOUGH.

YOU'RE JUST A FURRY ASSHOLE.

I ALWAYS FEEL LIKE I'M BEING WATCHED.

GOOD MORNING MISTER JAMES ABRAM.

WOULD YOU LIKE A SIP OF MY COFFEE?

YOU ARE ON DECAF FROM NOW ON!

CLOVER! WHAT ARE YOU DOING WITH MY MANUSCRIPT?!

I'M TRYING TO READ YOUR NOVEL!

WHY DOESN'T THIS BOOK HAVE ANY DRAGONS?!

HEY CLOVER! HOW DID YOU LIKE SKATEBOARDING?
GOOD!

I USED TO LOVE SKATING, BUT I QUIT AFTER I HAD AN EAR PROBLEM.
MY BALANCE WAS SO BAD! IT WAS HARD REALIZING I COULD NEVER BE A PRO SKATER NO MATTER HOW HARD I TRIED.

SO I SHOULD ONLY DO THINGS IF I CAN BE A PROFESSIONAL?

WHAT IS THIS WHINY MUSIC?
BEACH HOUSE?

AND IT'S ON VINYL TOO!
YOU'RE SUCH A POSER!

CAN YOU LEAVE ME ALONE?
I'M TRYING REALLY HARD TO RELAX RIGHT NOW.

YOU'RE POSING HARDER THAN THE MONA LISA.

GEEZ KEVIN!
WHAT DO YOU EVEN WANT?

OH YEAH!
CAN I BORROW TWENTY BUCKS?

I GOT TWENTY BUCKS, GONNA GET A PIZZA!
I GOT TWENTY BUCKS,
GONNA GET A PIZZA!

HOLD UP.
I COULD BUY SOMETHING AT THE GROCERY STORE AND HAVE EXTRA MONEY FOR THE REST OF THE WEEK.

RULES

WHO DOESN'T LOVE THE CALM BEFORE THEIR MORNIN' BREW?

WHO TOOK MY COFFEE?!

HEY MAN,
WHY THE LONG BEAK?

I WAS JUST TALKING TO MY NANA AND APPARENTLY SMOKING KILLED MY GREAT GRANDPA.

EVERYONE TOLD YOU IT WAS BAD WHEN YOU STARTED!
EVERYTHING ELSE YOU SAID WAS BAD ENDED UP BEING AWESOME!

WHAT DOES THE INTERNET SAY ABOUT IF A FELLA WANTS TO QUIT SMOKING?
LET ME CHECK.

MOVE OVER AND LET ME DO A SEARCH ON BING!

WHY ARE YOU ON FACEBOOK?
I'M ADDICTED TO THAT TOO!

PAPER

OH SHOOT!

SHORT CUT!
ANIME RULES

JUST LIKE SHAWSHANK!

I'M GONNA MAKE IT!

I MADE IT!!

HOW MUCH SILICON VALLEY DID I MISS?
STAN, IT'S SATURDAY.

THAT SHOW COMES ON TOMORROW.

PLEASE, KEEP WARM.

CLOSETS HAVE THE BEST STUFF!

OH COOL!

AN OLD TIMEY CALCULATOR!

CATMAN LOOKIT! I FOUND AN OLD CALCULATOR!

CLOVER, HOW CAN THIS BE A CALCULATOR?
HOW COULD YOU DO MATH WITH JUST TWO BUTTONS?

OH, THAT'S EASY!
IT'S FROM BACK WHEN MATH WAS SMALLER!

GAMEBOYS WERE HOW WE CARRIED GAMES PLACES WE DIDN'T NEED THEM BEFORE CELLPHONES.
AND GAMES CAME ON THESE CARTRIDGES BEFORE WE HAD CDS!

WHAT DID I SAY? WHY DO YOU LOOK CONFUSED?

WHAT IS A CD?

THIS GAMEBOY IS FINE; IT PROBABLY JUST NEEDS NEW BATTERIES.
I THINK WE HAVE SOME IN THE JUNK DRAWER.

WHAT'S TAKING YOU SO LONG CLOVER?

WE GOT A LOT OF JUNK!

HEY STAN?
WHAT KIDS DO FOR FUN BEFORE THEY INVENTED VIDEO GAMES?

CLOVER, I'VE ALWAYS HAD VIDEO GAMES.
YOU'RE PLAYING MY OLD GAMEBOY FROM WHEN I WAS A KID.

NO, BUT LIKE...
WHAT DID YOU DO BEFORE THEY WERE GOOD?

YOU ARE IN FOR A TREAT.
I COULDN'T STOP PLAYING POKEMON FOR EVEN AN INSTANT!

I WOULD STAY UP ALL NIGHT HIDING UNDER MY BLANKETS, PLAYING BY FLASHLIGHT!

OH MAN.
WE USED TO USE A LOT OF BATTERIES!

YOU KNOW, WHEN I WAS A KID WE DIDN'T HAVE CELLPHONES.
UH HUH.

SO WE WOULD ACTUALLY JUST GO PLACES,
AND JUST HOPE THAT SOMEONE WE KNEW SHOWED UP!

YEP.

AND SOMETIMES, YOU WOULD JUST HAVE TO TALK TO NEW PEOPLE!

YES STAN.

THAT IS VERY INTERESTING.

CAN I HAVE SOME CAKE?

SO MY BEST POKEMON IS SQUIRTLE, BUT I LIKE GEODUDE BECAUSE HE HAS COOL ARMS.
YEAH?

BUT I NEED A GRASS POKEMON, BUT NONE OF THEM ARE VERY CUTE.
AND I TRIED TO CATCH AN ABRA BUT HE JUST DISAPPEARED AND I COULDN'T CATCH HIM.

YEP.

AND THEN I TRIED TO FIGHT SOME GUYS ON A BRIDGE, AND THEN I BEAT THEM, AND THEN I GOT A GOLD NUGGET, AND THEN I SOLD IT FOR SOME POTIONS AND SOME POKEBALLS. SO NOW I HAVE A BUNCH OF POKEBALLS AND I HAVE A BUNCH OF POTIONS.

ALSO, STAN SAYS I HAVE TO ASK IF I CAN EAT YOUR CAKE.

HEY CLOVES!
I HEARD THROUGH THE GRAPEVINE THAT SOMEONE HAS BEEN TRYING OUT SOME CLASSIC VIDEO GAMES!

I PULLED ALL OF MY OLD GAMES OUT OF MY MOM'S HOUSE THIS MORNING.
COOL!

I EVEN BROUGHT MY OLD FAVORITE.
DOOM!
DOOM

IS THAT LIKE ZELDA?!
I GOT THE MAGIC HAMMER IN THAT!

KIND OF...

IT DOESN'T HAVE A MASTER SWORD, BUT THE CHAINSAW IS PRETTY CLOSE.

YOU HAVE SO MANY GAMES!
HOW DO YOU EVER CHOOSE WHAT TO PLAY?!
LIFE

I LIKE TO CONSIDER MY CURRENT MOOD AND GENERAL STATE OF MIND.
REALLY JUST FEEL OUT THE MOMENT.

AND THEN I USUALLY JUST PLAY FALLOUT.

HEY KEVIN, WHAT IS THE SIMS?
OH! IT'S GREAT! YOU HAVE THIS FAMILY,
AND YOU HAVE TO GET JOBS
AND MAKE SURE NO ONE DIES!

SO, IT'S JUST LIKE REAL LIFE?

YEAH!
IT'S PRETTY REALISTIC.

OKAY, CLOVER! IT'S TIME TO STOP BROWSING!
LET'S PLAY SOME THING!
LET'S PLAY DOOM!

A WISE CHOICE!

YOU READY?
LIFE SUCKS

READY!

NOW, I HAVE TO WARN YOU UP FRONT. DOOM IS A LITTLE SCARY.

IT'S GOT CUTE MONSTER MEN!!!

I HATE DOOM!
WHY IS THIS GAME SO STINKIN' HARD?!

CHALLENGE IS HALF THE FUN!
IF YOU MADE A GAME WHAT WOULD YOU DO DIFFERENTLY?

IT WOULD BE ABOUT PETTING A FLUFFY DOG!
OH! AND YOU EAT A CAKE!

AND THEN! AND THEN!
YOU CAN TAKE A NAP WITH THE DOG!

GO AWAY JAMES!
I'M BUSY RIGHT NOW!

THANK YOU FOR UNDERSTANDING.

SUNY

COME ON. THIS ISN'T ABOUT YOU.

I THOUGHT WE WERE BUDDIES.
PRETTY PLEASE SCOOT?

SUNY

CLOVER! CALM DOWN. IT'S JUST A GAME!

WAIT, ARE YOU CRYING?

WHAT? NO!
THIS GAME IS JUST HARD.

MY EYES ARE JUST SWEATY.

CLOVER, YOU HAVE TO CALM DOWN.
DOOM IS JUST A HARD GAME. YOU NEED TO BREATHE!

I CAN'T CALM DOWN KEVIN!
I KEEP GETTING SHOT!

THESE GUYS ARE DICKS.

WHOA CLOVES!
YOU CAN'T SAY THAT WORD.

WHY? YOU SAID IT EARLIER.

YOU LEARNED SOMETHING FROM ME?

I CAN'T BELIEVE CLOVER IS CURSING.
I KNEW SHE WAS TOO YOUNG FOR THOSE GAMES.

WHAT? NO.
SHE LEARNED IT FROM ME!

WHAT THE HECK KEVIN!
WHY DO YOU SEEM SO PROUD ABOUT THIS?!

ARE YOU KIDDING ME STAN?!
CHANGING A CHILD'S LIFE HAS SHOWED ME THERE IS PURPOSE IN THIS WORLD!

I GOTTA CALL MY GIRLFRIEND.
I THINK WE SHOULD HAVE A KID. OR JUST FIND ONE OR SOMETHING.

SO WHO WAS THAT GUY?

JUST SOME GUY.

WHY DID YOU SHOOT HIM?

I DUNNO.

DO YOU GET POINTS FOR SHOOTING HIM?
NO.

OH.

I GUESS HE DID LOOK PRETTY SHOOTABLE.

MAYBE YOU'RE SUPPOSED TO GO THROUGH THE OTHER DOOR.
I KNOW WHAT I'M DOING!

I KNOW, BUT MAYBE TRY THE OTHER DOOR NEXT TIME?
FINE.

SEE! IT WORKED!
SOMETIMES I KNOW WHAT I'M TALKING ABOUT.

COME ON, DON'T BE A JERK. WHAT ARE YOU DOING?

JUST CALLING THE NOBEL PRIZE COMMITTEE.

JUST CHECKING TO SEE IF THEY OFFER AWARDS FOR VIDEO GAME GENIUSES!

KIDS THESE DAYS ARE BEING RUINED BY ALL OF THESE VIDEO GAMES AND SNAPCHATS.
YEAH.

WE NEVER ACTED LIKE THESE LITTLE JERKS!
WAIT, WHAT?

ACK!

NICE SHIRT!
FUGAZI

COME ON CATMAN!
HOLD STILL!

BEDTIME? MORE LIKE DEAD TIME!

DOOM IS TOO HARD.
FUGAZI
SMILE

FUGAZI

I DON'T WANNA EAT ANY MORE WATER!
FUGAZI

DO YOU EVEN REMEMBER OUR CHILDHOOD?

BUT WE SAID PLEASE AND THANK YOU!

HEY CLOVES,
IT'S TIME TO TURN THE GAME OFF AND GO OUTSIDE FOR A LITTLE BIT.

NO.
THAT'S OKAY.

WHAT AM I SUPPOSED TO DO OUTSIDE?!
LOOK AT A TREE?
I KNOW WHAT A TREE LOOKS LIKE!

LET ME IN! LET ME IN! LET ME IN!!

BEING A SQUIRREL HAS TO BE FUN, RIGHT?
YOU GUYS ALWAYS SEEM SO CHIPPER.

WHAT DO YOU LIKE TO DO?
DO YOU HAVE ANY HOBBIES?

OH, I GET IT!
IT'S SOME SORT OF ZEN THING, ISN'T IT?!

WHAT ARE YOU LOOKING FOR?
WHAT'S IT LIKE TO LIVE SUCH A NATURAL UNATTACHED LIFESTYLE?

IS THIS WHERE YOU KEEP YOUR FOOD?

LIVING AT HOME IS SO STUPID.
I CAN'T EVEN DO WHATEVER I WANT.

I'M NEVER GOING HOME AGAIN EVER.

EXCEPT TO GO TO THE BATHROOM.
AND GET FRUIT SNACKS.

AND PROBABLY ON PANCAKE DAY.

WHERE ARE YOU GOING?
ARE THERE ACORNS OVER HERE?

OH MY GOSH!!

YOUR FRIENDS ARE SO COOL!

OH MY GOSH!!
HIS LITTLE VEST!

BAD APPLE

IT'S SO NICE OUT!
I WONDER HOW CLOVER IS DOING OUTSIDE.

MY TURN! MY TURN!

BE NICE TO OLD PEOPLE

HOLD UP!
WHERE ARE WE GOING?

EW, NO!
GUYS! YOU CAN'T DO THIS!!

EATING OUT OF THE TRASH IS GROSS!

HOLD UP...

IS THAT HALF A PIZZA?!

THIS IS THE ONLY WAY TO LIVE!
CHIRP CHIRP!

NO RULES.
NO BEDTIME.
ALL THE TRASH PIZZA YOU CAN EAT.

CHRIP, CHIRP CHIRP!

HA!
THAT IS SO TRUE!

COLLEGE IS FOR SUCKERS.

WHAT IS THIS?!

CHIRP!

FOR ME?
IS IT AN XBOX?!

OH MY GOSH...

PUNK VEST!
+10 TO LOOKING TOTALLY SWEET!

THIS IS SO COOL!
I LOOK LIKE I STINK!

HEY, COME ON GUYS. YOU NEED TO MOVE.

WHAT?
WHAT MAKES YOU THE BOSS OF THESE STEPS?
THIS IS MY HOUSE.
SO, PROBABLY THAT.
ANARCHY.

THIS IS THE ONLY WAY TO LIVE YOUR LIFE.
YEP.

JUST GOING WHEREVER THE OPEN ROAD TAKES YOU.

HEY! IT'S MY HOUSE!

HEY STAN!
HEY CLOVER! WHO ARE YOUR NEW FRIENDS?

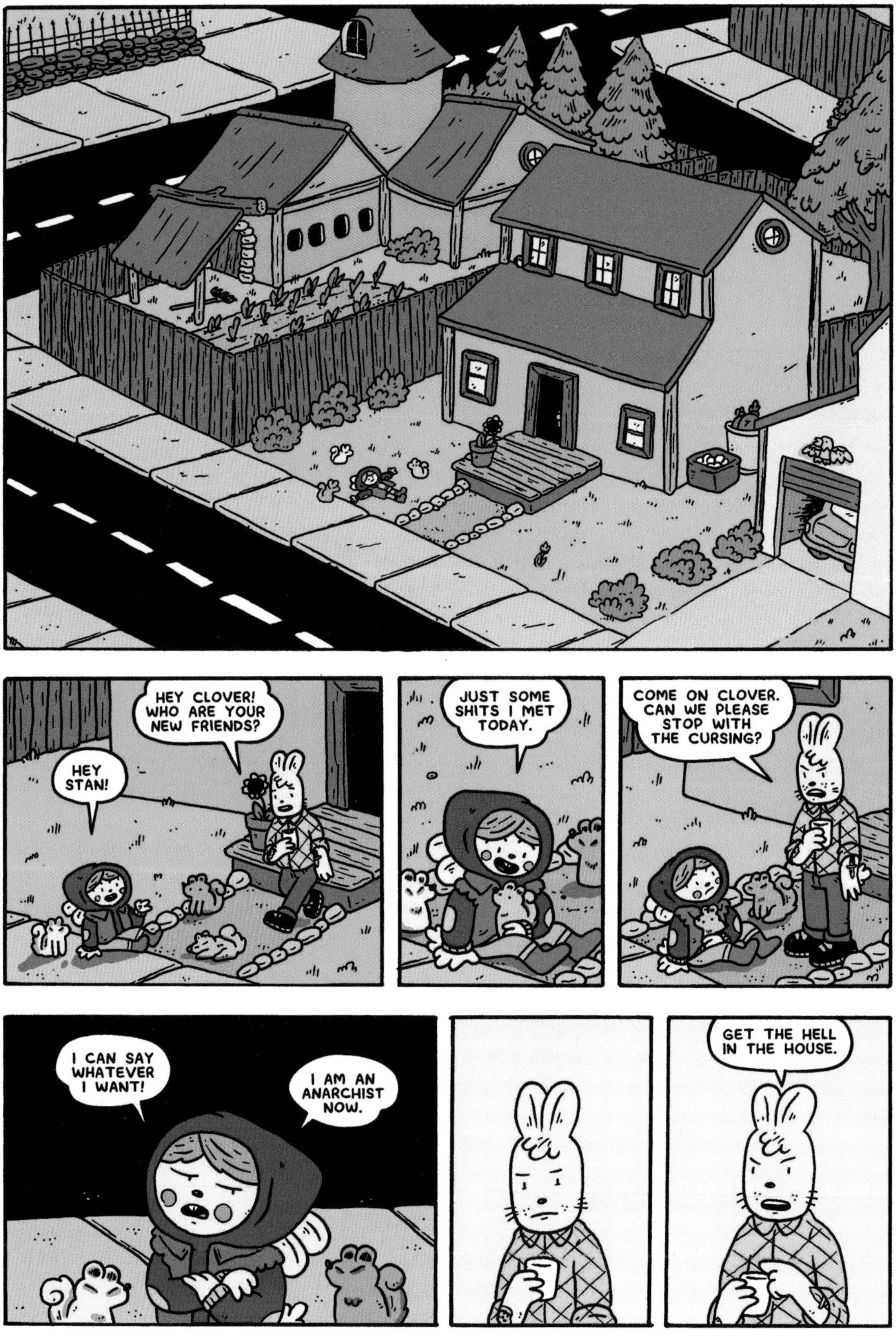

JUST SOME SHITS I MET TODAY.

COME ON CLOVER. CAN WE PLEASE STOP WITH THE CURSING?

I CAN SAY WHATEVER I WANT!
I AM AN ANARCHIST NOW.

GET THE HELL IN THE HOUSE.

GET IN THE HOUSE CLOVER!
NOW!

CHIRP!

GET OFF OF MY LAWN YOU LITTLE TREE RAT!

SHIT!
GETTING STABBED SUCKS!

WHY DO YOU GET TO SAY SHIT?!

DAMN IT CLOVER!
JUST GO INSIDE!

WHAT AM I SUPPOSED TO DO INSIDE?!

I DON'T CARE!
JUST PLAY A VIDEO GAME OR SOMETHING!

TODAY IS PRETTY GOOD.

WHAT ARE YOU PLAYING?
WIZARD QUEST FIVE.

I WAS TRYING TO SAVE THE PRINCESS FROM THE SKELETON WITCH, BUT NOW I THINK IT WAS A PLOY TO GET ME TO BRING THEM THE SKULL OF A THOUSAND NIGHTS AT THE DARKEST SWAMP CASTLE.
THAT WITCH IS REAL CRAFTY LIKE THAT.

WHAT?

THAT SOUNDS STUPID.

WHEN IS IT MY TURN?

SATURDAY MORNINGS.
THE PERFECT TIME TO CHILL OUT AND ENJOY THE COUCH AND SOME WIZARD'S QUEST!

IT'S MONDAY MORNING.
YOU'VE BEEN PLAYING FOR THE LAST THREE DAYS STRAIGHT.

ONE MORE LEVEL...

CAN YOU BELIEVE HOW MUCH TIME PEOPLE WASTE PLAYING THESE STUPID FANTASY GAMES?
YOU'VE BEEN PLAYING SINCE YOU WOKE UP THIS MORNING.
LITERALLY NONSTOP.

PLEASE HELP ME.

YOU KNOW WHAT?
I THINK VIDEO GAMES MIGHT BE ART.

THIS IS MORE THAN JUST POP CULTURE TRASH.
THIS IS THE REAL DEAL!

ARE YOU KIDDING ME? THIS FROM THE GUY WHO TOLD THE MUSEUM THEY NEEDED A JANITOR WHEN I TOOK YOU TO THAT POLLOCK SHOW?

YEAH, NO.
POLLOCK IS TRASH.

VIDEO GAMES RULE.

VIDEO GAMES RULE.

SO I HAVE TO SAVE THE PRINCE TO RESTORE ORDER TO THE KINGDOM?
YES.

OR, YOU CAN CAPTURE THE PRINCE AND RULE THE KINGDOM YOURSELF.
THERE ARE A LOT OF CHOICES, JUST LIKE REAL LIFE!

WHAT BUTTON DOES THE FIREBALL?

CAN I PLAY NOW?

FIVE MORE MINUTES.
YOU SAID THAT FIVE MINUTES AGO.

OH YEAH, SORRY.
TEN MORE MINUTES.

WHAT ARE YOU PLAYING?

CLOVER'S GAME WIZARD'S QUEST.
IT'S ABOUT WIZARDS, AND A QUEST, AND I THINK THERE IS A PRINCESS AND SOME GOLD OR SOMETHING?
I DON'T KNOW. THEY KEEP TALKING ABOUT HER WHEN I AM TRYING TO STAB UP SOME SKELETONS.

I THOUGHT YOU HATED VIDEO GAMES.
DIDN'T YOU SAY PEOPLE WHO PLAY GAMES ARE LAZY NERDS?

WHAT?
NO, THAT'S COMPLETELY DIFFERENT.

HOW IS IT ANY DIFFERENT?
THIS GAME HAS GOT SKELETONS IN IT.

CATMAN! IT'S TIME TO PUT DOWN THAT CONTROLLER AND GO OUTSIDE!
ONE MORE LEVEL!

YOU SAID ONE MORE LEVEL TWO DAYS AGO!
IT'S TIME TO TAKE A BREAK!

OKAY FINE!
JUST DON'T PLAY ON MY CHARACTER.

NOBODY IS GOING TO PLAY ON YOUR CHARACTER!
NOW GO OUTSIDE!

I CAN STOP PLAYING THE ELDER PRINCE AND SPEND THE NIGHT WITH A GOOD BOOK!

I DON'T HAVE A PROBLEM.
IT'S JUST A GAME.
I CAN QUIT WHENEVER I WANT!

BRAVE HERO! THE PRINCE REQUIRES YOUR ASSISTANCE!

HOLY COW!
YOU'VE GOTTEN SO MUCH READING DONE!

YOU REALLY SHOULD TREAT YOUR SELF.
MAYBE WITH A LITTLE VIDEO GAMING!

COME ON,
LEAVE ME ALONE.

I DON'T WANT TO PLAY VIDEO GAMES RIGHT NOW.
YEAH? WHAT ARE YOU READING?

A PEOPLE'S HISTORY OF VIDEO GAMING.

MAYBE YOU COULD PLAY A VIDEO GAME FOR A LITTLE BEFORE BED!
YOU KNOW, A LITTLE TREAT FOR YOUR SELF!
SORRY IMAGINARY MOUSE, I HAVE TO GET UP EARLY IN THE MORNING.

TO PLAY VIDEO GAMES?

GOODNIGHT LITTLE FELLA.

LAST NIGHT WAS SO WEIRD. I REALLY NEED TO CUT BACK ON MY VIDEO GAMING.
THAT LITTLE WIZARD MOUSE HALLUCINATION KEPT ME UP ALL NIGHT WITH HIS BLABBERING ABOUT MY QUEST TO SAVE THE PRINCE.

MAYBE I SHOULD CUT BACK ON MY SUGAR TOO.

BRAVE HERO, YOU HAVE AWOKEN! I BRING WORD FROM THE PRINCE!

LITTLE GUY, YOU HAVE TO STOP. YOU AREN'T EVEN REAL.
ALSO, I DON'T KNOW IF IT'S OKAY TO EAT FOOD IF THE MOUSE THAT WAS IN IT IS IMAGINARY.

I DON'T THINK I CAN PLAY THIS GAME ANYMORE. I AM PHYSICALLY EXHAUSTED.

ALSO, I THINK LOOKING AT THE SCREEN IS MAKING ME SEASICK.

NO! YOU MUST CONTINUE BRAVE WARRIOR!

THE FUTURE OF THE TEN KINGDOMS IS IN YOUR STRONG AND CAPABLE HANDS!
YOU CAN'T LET US DOWN! IT IS YOUR DESTINY TO BRING ORDER TO THE REALMS!

I DON'T KNOW MAN.
THIS IS A LOT OF PRESSURE.
AND I STILL HAVEN'T EVEN FED THE CAT TODAY.

OKAY. I THINK I REALLY HAVE TO STOP PLAYING. MY VISION IS GETTING ALL SHAKY AND THINK I MIGHT BE HAVING A STROKE.

YOU MUST RESIST THE TEMPTATION TO QUIT NO MATTER HOW MUCH SUFFERING YOU HAVE TO ENDURE!
A GREAT CHAMPION WOULD NEVER GIVE UP UNDER SUCH A TRIVIAL OBSTACLE AS A LITTLE LACK OF SLEEP!

I GUESS YOU ARE RIGHT.

MAYBE I CAN JUST TAKE A QUICK NAP.

DON'T EVEN THINK ABOUT IT!
IF YOU CLOSE YOUR EYES FOR EVEN A SECOND I WILL END YOU!

THIS IS THE LAST STRAW LITTLE FELLA!
THIS VIDEO GAME DOESN'T OWN ME!
AND YOU CAN'T TELL ME WHAT TO DO!
WHAT ARE YOU GOING TO DO?

YOU CAN'T HURT ME. DON'T YOU REMEMBER? I AM NOT EVEN REAL!

I KNOW WHAT I HAVE TO DO.

WHAT WAS THAT NOISE?

WHAT IS ALL THIS GREY PLASTIC ON THE FLOOR? IS THAT THE NINTENDO?!

I LOVE YOU?

GEEZ CATMAN.
WHAT HAPPENED HERE?

STAN! IT WAS TERRIBLE!
THERE WAS THIS LITTLE WIZARD MOUSE!
AND I HAD TO SAVE THE TEN KINGDOMS!
AND SAVE THE PRINCE FROM THE DARK LORD AND HIS ONCOMING HORDES!

I DON'T KNOW WHAT ANY OF THAT MEANS.
DO YOU WANT SOME BREAK-FAST?

I ALREADY HAD SOME BREAKFAST.

YOU WANT ANOTHER ONE?
YES.

WHY DOES CATMAN LOOK SO TIRED?
IS HE SICK?

CATMAN HAD A LONG NIGHT.
I AM NOT SURE WHAT HAPPENED, BUT HE SMASHED UP THE NINTENDO PRETTY GOOD.

OH, OKAY.

SMASH THE SYSTEM!

I AM GOING TO GO HIDE MY DREAMCAST.

BEING A WRITER IS SO DIFFICULT.
HOW AM I SUPPOSED TO WRITE EVERY SINGLE DAY?

YOU ARE SO BLESSED WITH YOUR SIMPLE LIFE.

IF I DON'T FIND ENOUGH BREAD CRUMBS TODAY I WILL LITERALLY DIE TOMORROW.

HAVE YOU EVER CONSIDERED QUITTING SMOKING?
IT'S SO BAD FOR YOU!

YOU EAT ICE CREAM AND THAT'S NOT GOOD FOR YOU EITHER!
THAT'S NOT THE SAME THING AT ALL!

YOU'RE RIGHT!
NOBODY LOOKS BADASS WITH A BOWL OF ICE CREAM IN THEIR FACE.

HEY, STAN! WHAT ARE YA' LISTENING TOO?

JUST BURZUM! IT'S SO GOOD!

UNDER OATH
TRACK 3
MENU

WHAT ARE YOU DOING?
WHY DO YOU LOOK SO HAPPY?

JUST DRINKING TEA AND SITTING.

OK,
THIS IS PRETTY NICE.

PLEASE KEEP WARM!
WHERE IS IT?!

HAVE EITHER OF YOU SEEN MY LUCKY RED PEN?
I TOOK THE DAY OFF TO WORK ON THE OLD NOVEL, BUT I CAN'T FIND IT ANYWHERE.
NO, BUT I HAVE A BLUE ONE IF YOU NEED IT.

WHAT?
HOW AM I SUPPOSED TO WRITE WITH A BLUE PEN?
I AM SEVEN.

STAN, I DON'T GET IT.
WHY CAN'T YOU JUST WRITE WITH A NORMAL PEN?
COME ON!
YOU KNOW I CAN'T WRITE WITHOUT THE RED ONE.
WAS IT RED?

YES!
HAVE YOU SEEN IT?
YES.
I THINK.

OH, THANK YOU GOSH!

WHERE IS IT?!

I AM SEVEN YEARS OLD.

CHECK IT OUT!

YOU THOUGHT I WAS WASTING MY TIME! HA!

I FOUND IT!

THAT'S NOT MY RED PEN!
IT'S MY FRISBEE!

IT'S NOT ALWAYS ABOUT YOU STAN!

I GUESS I WILL NEVER WRITE MY NOVEL NOW...

OH MAN.
IT'S IN YOUR POCKET, ISN'T IT?!

I DON'T WANT TO TALK ABOUT IT!
HA HA!
HAHA HA!
I'M SEVEN!

JAW BREA KER
FINALLY. I CAN GET TO WORK!
EVERYTHING IN ITS RIGHT PLACE.

I NEED A COFFEE!

PLEASE, KEEP WARM.

PLEASE KEEP WARM!
PEW PEW!!
WHAT DO YOU WANT FOR BREAKFAST CLOVER?
DO OMELETTES SOUND GOOD?

YES PLEASE!
WITH PEPPERS PLEASE!

WHAT THE HECK?

IT'S MY ROCK COLLECTION!

CLOVER!
WHERE ARE THE EGGS?!
THIS ONE LOOKS LIKE YOU!

CLOVER.
I NEED YOU TO TELL ME WHERE YOU PUT THE EGGS.

I HID THEM!

WHAT DO YOU MEAN YOU HID THEM?

YOU KNOW, LIKE EASTER? WITH THE RABBIT AND ALL THAT STUFF?

CLOVER.
HOW MANY EGGS WERE IN THERE?
IT WAS FULL!

SNAKE THE BAND.

HEY, WHAT ARE YOU GUYS UP TOO?
HEY KEVIN.
CLOVER DECIDED TODAY WAS GOING TOO WELL FOR EVERYONE.
I'M IN TROUBLE!

HA! THIS IS WHY YOU'RE A SUCKER FOR HAVING A KID AROUND.

DIDN'T YOU JUST SAY THAT YOU AND YOUR GIRLFRIEND WERE TALKING ABOUT HAVING A KID?

HUH?

OH YEAH.
WE BROKE UP.
WATER MUSIC
EGGS COME FROM BIRDS!

SORRY ABOUT YOUR GIRLFRIEND, BUT WE ARE HERE FOR YOU.
JUST LET US KNOW IF THERE IS ANYTHING WE CAN DO.

CAN I CRASH HERE FOR A FEW DAYS?

NOPE.

END!

I'M WORRIED CLOVER IS GETTING TOO MUCH SCREEN TIME.

HEY, CLOVER?
HOW ARE YOU FEELING?

I'M BORED.

HEY THERE CLOVER!
CATMAN AND I HAVE DECIDED WE SHOULD ALL GO OUT CAMPING!

THAT SOUNDS VERY NICE!
HAVE A GOOD TIME!

NO, IT'S GOING TO BE A FAMILY TRIP!
YOU GET TO COME TOO!

OH, COME ON.
WHY DON'T YOU LOOK EXCITED?

I AM VERY EXCITED, TO SPEND TIME WITH NO WIFI OR A BATHROOM.
JUST LOOK AT MY BIG SMILE.

HEY STAN, ARE WE ALL PACKED UP AND READY TO GO?

YES SIR! FOOD, WATER, SOME LITTLE MARSHMALLOWS.
THE TENT, SLEEPING BAGS.
CLOVER.

LET ME OUT!
LET ME OUT!
I DON'T WANNA GO CAMPING!

THE CITY CAN REALLY WEAR DOWN ON THE SPIRIT.

SPENDING A LITTLE TIME IN THE WOODS CAN HELP YOU LET OFF SOME OF THE STRESS.

I THINK I FEEL REFRESHED ALREADY!

NOW WATCH WHAT I DO.
YOU HAVE TO SET UP YOUR OWN TENT.
OKAY.

CLOVER, COME ON.
IT'S VERY IMPORTANT THAT YOU ARE PAYING ATTENTION TO WHAT I AM DOING!

SHOOT.
WHAT DID I DO?
IT'S A PUPPY!

HEY CLOVER? CAN YOU HELP GET SOME STICKS FOR THE CAMPFIRE?

WHERE AM I SUPPOSED TO FIND STICKS IN THE WOODS?!

I'M PRETTY GOOD AT CAMPING.

HEY CLOVER, DO YOU WANT TO COME DOWN TO THE LAKE WITH ME AND CATMAN?
NO THANK YOU.

COME ON!
DON'T YOU WANT TO SEE SOME OF THE LOCAL SIGHTS?

NO THANK YOU.

COME ON, WE NEED YOU!
WE DON'T WANT TO BE ALONE.

I THINK YOU BOYS ARE RESPONSIBLE ENOUGH TO GO ON WITHOUT ME.

LEMME DOWN! LEMME DOWN!
WE NEED SOMEONE RESPONISIBLE TO WATCH US.

WOW!
IT'S SO NICE OUT! I TOLD YOU THIS WOULD BE A GOOD TIME.

YOU'RE NOT THE BOSS OF ME.

DO A BIG SPLASH!

THIS IS PERFECT!

WHERE IS EVERY ONE?

I WONDER IF PEOPLE HATE ME OR IF I'M JUST BORING.

MAYBE I JUST DON'T ASSERT MYSELF ENOUGH.

NO. THEY DEFINITELY HATE ME.

HEY FLOWER.
WHAT ARE YOU UP TO?

THINKING ABOUT DEATH.

OH. THAT'S WEIRD.
DO YOU HAVE ANY FOOD?

YOU KNOW WHAT HELPS ME WHEN I'M SAD?
FOOD!

I'M NOT REALLY SAD. JUST KIND OF DEPRESSED.

OH! YOU KNOW WHAT ALWAYS HELPS ME WHEN I'M KIND OF DEPRESSED?
FOOD?
OKAY, YOU KNOW WHERE THIS IS GOING.

YOU CAN'T LET IT BOTHER YOU. PEOPLE FORGET TO INVITE ME TO STUFF ALL THE TIME!

IT DOESN'T MEAN NOTHIN'!

KEVIN.
PEOPLE DON'T INVITE YOU TO THINGS BECAUSE YOU ARE KIND OF DISAGREEABLE.

HMMM... NO.
I DON'T THINK THAT'S TRUE.

I'M NOT DISAGREEABLE!

I AGREE THAT S'MORES ARE THE BEST DESSERT OF ALL TIME!

ICE CREAM IS MY FAVORITE DESSERT.
EW! GROSS.

FLOWER. DO YOU HAVE ANYTHING TO DRINK HERE?

WHAT DO YOU THINK WOULD GO WELL WITH S'MORES?

I BELIEVE IT WOULD PAIR WELL WITH A LEMON SELTZER.
OR THIS DIET SPRITE FROM THE BACK OF THE VEGGIE SHELF.

GEEZ.
JUST SAY I'M NOT DISAGREEABLE AND WE CAN AGREE TO DISAGREE.

KEVIN!
THAT'S NOT WHAT AGREE TO DISAGREE MEANS!

WHAT? YEAH IT IS!
BUT WE CAN AGREE TO DISAGREE.

THE WOODS ARE A BIG WASTE OF SPACE.
THERE IS NOTHING OUT HERE!

THERE IS SOMETHING OUT HERE!

OH MAN!
HOW COULD THIS POSSIBLY GO WRONG?!

A WARM FIRE. A LITTLE BED. IT'S SO COZY!

IT'S LIKE OUT OF A BOOK.

LIKE GOLDILOCKS OR SOMETHING!

OH NO!

I GOTTA FIND THE SOUP AND GET OUTTA HERE!

WHAT THE HECK?
I THOUGHT THE CAMP WAS OVER HERE!

I'VE PASSED THIS ROCK LIKE FIVE TIMES ALREADY!

WHY DOES EVERYTHING IN MY LIFE TYRY TO CONFUSE ME?!

LOOK AT YOU NOW CLOVER, LOST IN THE WOODS ALL ALONE.
I GOTTA FIND MORE FOOD. THIS CAN OF SOUP WON'T LAST MORE THAN A WEEK.

THINK CLOVER THINK!

WAIT! I CHANGED MY MIND! DON'T FALL FOR MY TRAP!
WE CAN SHARE THE SOUP!

DO YOU HAVE A CAN OPENER?

CAN YOU BELIEVE I WAS SCARED OF THE WOODS? IT CAN'T BE TOO BAD.

IF A CUTE GUY LIKE YOU LIVES HERE.

THIS IS A NEIGHBORHOOD WHERE YOU COULD RAISE A FAMILY!

IF WE ARE GOING TO STARVE I WANT YOU TO EAT ME FIRST.

YOU'RE RIGHT.

WE SHOULD PROBABLY WAIT UNTIL THE SOUP IS GONE BEFORE WE HAVE THIS CONVERSATION.

WOW!
THIS CAMPING TRIP IS THE MOST PLEASANT THING WE HAVE DONE THIS YEAR.

YEAH, IT'S SO QUIET. I CAN HEAR THE BIRDS!

WHERE IS CLOVER?!

GOOD JOB!
DID YOU FIND SOME BERRIES?!

OH NO!

YOU'RE RIGHT...
THIS IS ABOUT SURVIVAL.

CLOVER! I AM SO GLAD TO SEE YOU! WE HAVE BEEN LOOKING EVERYWHERE FOR YOU.

ARE YOU EATING BUGS?
YOU'VE ONLY BEEN OUT HERE FOR AN HOUR!

IT'S NOT MY FAULT!
SHE MADE IT LOOK SO COOL!

YOU CAN'T JUST WALK OFF INTO THE WOODS LIKE THAT!
IT'S DANGEROUS OUT HERE!

IT'S NOT DANGEROUS! IF IT WAS DANGEROUS HOW COULD EMILY LIVE HERE?!

I DON'T THINK YOU SHOULD BE HANGING OUT WITH RODENTS ANYMORE.

NO WAY.
SHE AIN'T DANGEROUS!

HER TEETH ARE TOO LITTLE.

HEY STAN?
WHY ARE SOME FLOWERS BIGGER THAN OTHERS?

SOME FLOWERS JUST TAKE A LITTLE LONGER THAN OTHERS TO GROW!
SOMEDAY YOU WILL BE BIG TOO!

WEIRD.

STAN, WHEN ARE WE GOING TO GO HOME?
CLOVER, WE ARE CAMPING TONIGHT.

SO LIKE AN HOUR?

FLOWER, YOU NEED TO BE MORE CHILL. LIKE ME. ICE COLD!
OH NO KEVIN.
I ASSURE YOU, I AM VERY CHILL.

IF YOU'RE SO CHILL THEN WHY DIDN'T YOU GET INVITED ON THE CAMPING TRIP EVERYONE IS AWAY ON?

WAIT, THEY INVITED YOU ON THE TRIP?

I MEAN I WASN'T INVITED, BUT AT LEAST THEY TOLD ME. GEEZ.
I TOLD YOU, I AM VERY CHILL.
GO FISH.

YOU KNOW WHAT? MAYBE WE SHOULD HAVE A LITTLE GET TOGETHER!

OH NO!
WE HAVE TO TIDY UP FIRST!

MAYBE WE COULD INVITE THAT CUTE WIZARD COUPLE FROM DOWN THE STREET!

BUT JUST A FEW PEOPLE!

WE DID IT!
OH NO!

KEVIN, THIS IS TOO MANY PEOPLE!
SOMEONE IS GOING TO BREAK SOMETHING IMPORTANT!

FLOWER, CHILL! IT'S A PARTY! HAVE A GOOD TIME. WHY DON'T YOU GO TALK TO KYLER?

IS HE SMOKING IN THE HOUSE?!
DIDN'T I JUST SAY YOU SHOULD CHILL? SOMETIMES I FEEL LIKE YOU DON'T EVEN LISTEN TO ME.

HEY GUYS? I AM VERY SORRY TO BE SUCH A SPOIL SPORT.
BUT CAN WE PLEASE NOT TATTOO IN MY KITCHEN?

SORRY, I AM ALREADY DONE.

MOTHER
SHUCKER

HOW CAN PEOPLE GO INTO ANOTHER PERSON'S HOME AND BE SO MESSY?
HEY!

I'M TRYING TO NAP OVER HERE!

WELL I AM SORRY! HOW SILLY OF ME TO ASSUME I CAN USE MY OWN TRASH CAN!
IT WOULDN'T HURT FOR YOU TO CHILL OUT JUST A LITTLE.

HEY FLOWER.
NO ONE SHOULD EVER LOOK THIS STRESSED AT THEIR OWN PARTY!

I'M NOT STRESSED AT ALL!
I'M HAVING A VERY RELAXED SIT DOWN IN THE CORNER!
I'M VERY CHILL!

I GUESS YOU ARE RIGHT! MY MISTAKE! GOOD TALK!

TIME FOR S'MORES!
YOU READY FOR S'MORES CLOVER?
WHAT ARE S'MORES?

WHAT ARE S'MORES?
YOU'RE KILLIN' ME SMALLS!

GREAT REFERENCE!
THANKS!
YOU KNOW I FEEL LEFT OUT WHEN YOU MAKE LITERARY REFERENCES!

OKAY CLOVER.
A S'MORE IS A TOASTED MARSHMALLOW WITH CHOCOLATE BETWEEN TWO PIECES OF GOLDEN GRAHAM CRACKERS.
YOU'RE GOING TO LOVE IT!

SO A S'MORE IS JUST A SANDWICH?
I GUESS YOU COULD SAY THAT, YEAH.

IT'S TOO LATE TO EAT THAT!!
SANDWICHES ARE A LUNCH TIME FOOD!

I LIKE MY S'MORES A LITTLE BIT BURNT. IT GIVES IT THAT AUTHENTIC SMOKY CAMPFIRE FLAVOR.

PERSONALLY, I LIKE MINE SLIGHTLY TOASTED.
BUT YOU SHOULD FOLLOW YOUR BLISS!

OKAY.
MAYBE NEXT TIME YOUR BLISS COULD LEAD YOU TO AT LEAST PUT IT NEAR THE FIRE FOR A FEW SECONDS.

CLOVER CAN REALLY PUT THOSE S'MORES BACK!
RIGHT?
I DON'T THINK I'VE EVER SEEN HER THIS CONTENT!

YEAH.
I THINK I MIGHT DO THE ALL S'MORE DIET THIS YEAR.

ALRIGHT.
LET'S SEE IF WE CAN GET YOU EATING VEGETABLES REGULARLY BEFORE WE TRY ANY FAD DIETS.

ALRIGHT, I HOPE YOU ARE READY FOR THIS CLOVER.
THE MOST IMPORTANT PART OF THE CAMPING EXPERIENCE!
IS IT AS GOOD AS S'MORES?!

IT'S TIME FOR SCARY STORIES!

CAT MAN!
STOP WASTING BATTERIES LIKE THAT! I NEED THEM FOR MY GAMEBOY!

AND WHEN THEY RETURNED TO THE COMPUTER LAB ON THAT DARK STORMY NIGHT...
THE PAST HAD COME BACK TO HAUNT THEM...
ALL OF THEIR DEFAULT BROWSERS HAD BEEN REPLACED... BY NETSCAPE NAVIGATOR!

IS NETSCAPE SOME KIND OF GHOST OR SOMETHING?!

IT IS NOW.

AND WHEN THEY ARRIVED SAFELY IN THE DRIVEWAY...
THERE WAS A HOOK HANGING FROM THEIR CAR DOOR!
THAT'S NOT EVEN SCARY!
LET ME TRY!!

I THINK I GET THE GIST OF HOW THIS SCARY STORY THING WORKS.

AND WHEN THEY GOT HOME FROM THE SCARY WOODS, THE BATTERIES WERE ALL DEAD!
SO THEY COULDN'T PLAY THEIR GAMEBOY!

OKAY YOU GUYS.
I THINK IT MIGHT BE TIME TO HIT THE HAY.

HOW ABOUT JUST ONE MORE STORY?
SO YOU ADMIT THAT YOU LIKE CAMPING?

I DON'T HAVE TO ADMIT ANYTHING!
GOODNIGHT CLOVER!

MOMENTS WHEN YOU REMEMBER YOU ARE ALIVE ARE REALLY IMPORTANT.
IT'S A GIFT, YOU KNOW?

BURP!

THE INTERNET IS JUST LIKE THE MATRIX! HAVEN'T YOU EVER THOUGHT ABOUT IT LIKE THAT?!
IT'S MAKING US ONE BIG BRAIN!

CHIRP CHIRP!

I THINK MAYBE YOU HAVE HAD TOO MUCH TO DRINK!

HEY FLOWER?
YOU DOING OKAY DOWN THERE?
GO AWAY. I'M BUSY.

YOU DON'T LOOK BUSY.

HOW WOULD YOU EVEN KNOW WHAT BUSY LOOKS LIKE?

YOU KNOW.
IT'S FUNNY YOU SAY THAT.

I'VE BEEN THINKING A LOT ABOUT THE POSSIBILITIES OF PRODUCTION AS AN ANTI-CAPITALIST ACT.

YOU AREN'T GOING TO LEAVE ME ALONE, ARE YOU?

THIS IS A PRETTY GREAT PARTY, EVEN IF IT IS A LITTLE ROWDY.
WHY CAN'T YOU JUST RELAX AND ENJOY THE MOMENT?

YOU REALLY DON'T GET IT DO YOU?

YOU ALWAYS RUN HEAD FIRST INTO EVERYTHING WITHOUT PAYING ANY ATTENTION TO HOW ANYONE ELSE FEELS ABOUT IT.

IT WOULDN'T BE A PROBLEM IF YOU WEREN'T SO CHARMING.

YOU THINK I'M CHARMING?
I THINK YOU SHOULDN'T PUSH IT.

WHAT DO YOU SAY WE SHUT THIS PARTY DOWN?
MAYBE WE CAN LET IT GO ON A BIT LONGER.
IT SEEMS TO BE UNDER CONTROL.

HEY, IS THIS YOUR PARTY?
YES. YES IT IS.

COOL COOL.
THE COPS ARE OUT FRONT.

HOLY CRAP, IT'S THE COPS!
DAMN IT KEVIN! I TOLD YOU THE PARTY WAS TOO BIG!

DON'T WORRY, IT'S NOT A BIG DEAL. IT'S PROBABLY JUST A NOISE COMPLAINT.
LIFE SUCKS

ARE THEY CARRYING A KEG?!

WHAT'S THE EASIEST WAY TO END A PARTY?
I THINK YOU JUST HAVE TO DO IT.
LIKE A BAND AID.

OH YEAH, LIKE A BAND AID!
YOU GET IT!
WHAT ARE YOU WAITING FOR?

OH, I USUALLY GET SOMEONE ELSE TO PULL MINE OFF.
I THOUGHT YOU WERE OFFERING TO DO IT.

PARTY'S OVER!
YOU DON'T HAVE TO GO HOME BUT YOU CAN'T STAY HERE!

IT'S CLOSING TIME NOW SEMISONIC.
STOP PUSHING ME, I'M LEAVING.

SORRY DAVE. I DON'T REALLY KNOW HOW OTHER PEOPLE GET ASKED TO LEAVE PARTIES.
CALL ME TOMOROW!

HEY GUYS.
WE ARE WRAPPING IT UP!
OKAY, NO WORRIES.

HOLD UP.
DID YOUR DOG JUST TALK?
NOPE. I'M JUST PRACTICING MY VENTRILOQUISM.

OH, COOL. THAT'S A NEAT TRICK!
WHAT A DORK.
I'M GOING TO POOP IN HIS YARD.

THANK YOU GUYS SO MUCH FOR COMING!
IT WAS GREAT MEETING YOU!

CHIRP!
CHIRP, CHIRP.

WHAT DID THE RATTY RODENT SAY?
THEY INVITED ME OVER FOR ACORNS AND TEA.

I THINK THAT IS THE LAST PARTY I WILL EVER HAVE.

WELL, GREAT SHIN DIG!
THANKS FOR HAVING ME!

OKAY, I WILL SEE YOU AROUND.
OKAY FINE!
I WILL STAY AND HELP CLEAN!

IT'S SO WEIRD THAT SOME PEOPLE DON'T RECYCLE.
IT'S SO SIMPLE!

I DON'T MEAN TO OFFEND YOU, BUT YOU DON'T REALLY STRIKE ME AS A RECYCLER.

OH, I DON'T RECYCLE.
I NEED MY CARDBOARD FOR FORT RELATED PROJECTS.

IT FEELS PRETTY DANG GOOD TO CLEAN UP THIS MUCH STUFF.
YEAH, I GUESS.
WE DID FORGET A PRETTY CRUCIAL STEP.

YOU MEAN TAKING IT OUTSIDE?

NOPE. LEAF PILE STUFF!
LIFE SUCKS

DID YOU MEAN IT WHEN YOU SAID YOU THOUGHT I WAS CHARMING?
I GUESS I DID MEAN IT, EVEN IF I DIDN'T MEAN TO SAY IT.

IT'S JUST NICE THAT YOU WEREN'T WEIRD ABOUT IT OR ANYTHING.

DO YOU WANT TO KISS OR SOMETHING?
NO. THAT'S OKAY.

YAWN!

SHOOT!
I BET IT WAS THAT RACCOON!!

CATMAN! SOMETHING GOT INTO OUR CAMP LAST NIGHT!

OH, NO! WHERE IS CLOVER?!

ZZZZ!

WHAT THE HECK CLOVER?!
YOU ATE EVERYTHING WE PACKED FOR OUR BREAKFAST!

DON'T YOU HAVE ANYTHING TO SAY FOR YOURSELF?
THIS ISN'T FAIR!

YOU ARE THE ONE WHO ATE ALL OF THE FOOD!
WHAT ISN'T FAIR ABOUT THIS?

I'M GETTING IN TROUBLE FOR EATING EVERYTHING AND IT WASN'T EVEN GOOD.

SWEET HOME.

IT'S PERFECT!

HEY
THERE
FLOWER.
YOU DOING
ALRIGHT?

OF COURSE
I AM STAN.
WHY WOULDN'T
I BE OKAY?

I THOUGHT YOU MIGHT BE
DEHYDRATED FROM ALL OF
THE DROOL YOU LOST.
OH.
GROSS.

SO, CAN I
CALL YOU
TOMORROW?
WHY?
YOU ARE ALWAYS
HERE EATING OUR
FOOD ANYWAYS.
OKAY.

HEY
KEVIN?

YEAH?
THAT WOULD
BE NICE.

THIS WEEKEND HAS
BEEN A REAL TRIP.
MAYBE I SHOULD
TRY TO POUR THAT
ENERGY INTO WORKING
ON MY NOVEL A LITTLE
BIT TONIGHT!

OR WE
COULD WATCH
DIE HARD.

STAN? CAN WE MAKE
SMORES AGAIN?
OR MAYBE
WE COULD
WATCH THE
SECOND
DIE HARD!

NOT NOW
CLOVER.
TODAY IS
OVER.
OH.
OK.

NIGHT!
10:10

PLEASE KEEP WARM

CRUNCH!
MUNCH!
CRUNCH!

HACK

COUGH! HACK

HACK!
PEW!

I NEED TO BE MORE CAREFUL!
I COULD HAVE DIED!

CRUNCH
MUNCH

OKAY ME.
IF I AM GOING TO WRITE A NOVEL I HAVE TO KNOW WHAT IT'S ABOUT BEFORE I GET STARTED.
PUNK

FIRST I NEED A CHARACTER WHO IS LIKEABLE, BUT NOT TOO COOL.

AND MAYBE A RELATABLE LOCATION.

AND THEY SHOULD BE DOING SOMETHING I HAVE SOME EXPERIENCE WITH SO I CAN WRITE IT WELL!

OH.
NOVEL IDEA

CAPTN
COOKIE

YES!
I DID IT!
CAPTN
COOKIE

THE FIRST OLYMPICS WERE IN 776 BC !

THEY HAD RUNNING!
AND WRESTLING, AND PROBABLY OTHER COOL STUFF TOO!

NOW THEY HAVE EVEN BETTER STUFF!
STUFF LIKE SNOWBOARDS AND BOWLING!

HEY CLOVER, I DON'T KNOW IF WE SHOULD BE RUNNING IN THE HOUSE.
BUT YOU SAID IF A PERSON WANTS TO GET GOOD AT A THING THEY HAVE TO PRACTICE ALL THE TIME!

COPS

STAR WARS IS ALRIGHT I GUESS.

MOVING BACKWARDS
LS
TTYL!

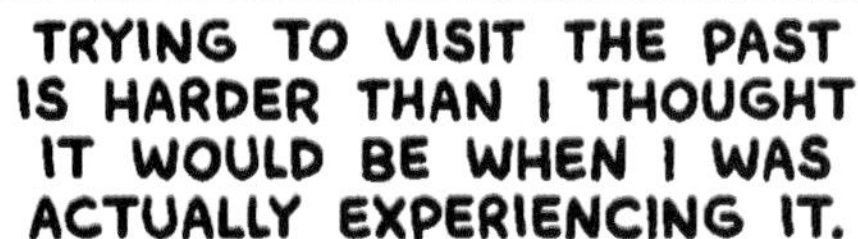
TRYING TO VISIT THE PAST IS HARDER THAN I THOUGHT IT WOULD BE WHEN I WAS ACTUALLY EXPERIENCING IT.

YOU ARE HERE

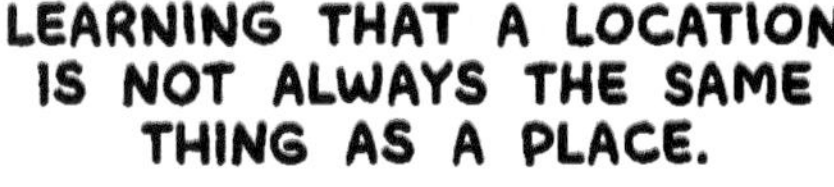
LEARNING THAT A LOCATION IS NOT ALWAYS THE SAME THING AS A PLACE.

YOU CAN'T GO BACK,

TO WHERE YOU'VE BEEN BEFORE.

DIGGING AROUND IN THE PAST HAS BEEN GETTING WEIRD LATELY.

I DON'T KNOW WHY, BUT EVEN POSITIVE MEMORIES ARE STARTING TO BOTHER ME.

SOMETIMES I FEEL LIKE THE PAST WANTS TO EAT ME ALIVE.

LIVE!
5$
IT DOESNT TAKE MUCH TO REMIND ME THAT
this isnt
WHAT I THOUGHT IT WOULD BE LIKE TO GET
WHAT I WANTED

AM I ENVIOUS OF MY OLD YOUNGER SELF?

IT'S NOT LIKE I WANT TO GO BACK.

THINGS ARE BETTER NOW THAN THEY HAVE EVER BEEN BEFORE.

PLEASE KEEP WARM!
HEY FLOWER!
WHY ARE YOU PLAYING WITH YARD DIRT?

HEY THERE CLOVER.
I'M NOT PLAYING. I'M GROWING US FOOD!
DO YOU WANT US TO GROW ANYTHING SPECIFIC?

RANCH FLAVORED SUNFLOWER SEEDS ARE PRETTY GOOD.
YOU SHOULD PLANT SOME OF THOSE.

THAT'S NOT REALLY HOW IT WORKS.

OH, OKAY.
SPICY HOT SEEDS ARE GOOD TOO I GUESS.

NATURE IS MAGIC.
IF WE GIVE THESE TOMATOES ENOUGH WATER AND THEY GET ENOUGH SUN WE CAN EAT THEM FOR DINNER A FEW NIGHTS A WEEK.
SEED TIME

THAT SOUNDS STUPID.

VEGETABLES COME FROM THE GROCERY STORE.

WHAT'S UP YOU GUYS?
GETTING SOME VITAMIN D?

NOTHING.
FLOWER THINKS VEGETABLES ARE MADE OUT OF DIRT.

HOLD UP.
VEGETABLES GROW IN THE DIRT, AND THEN WE EAT THEM?

YES!

OH.

WELL I GUESS THAT SETTLES IT.

I'M NOT EATING VEGETABLES ANYMORE!

HEY
LITTLE
CLOVER.
WHAT ARE
YOU CRYING
ABOUT?
I JUST FOUND
OUT VEGETABLES
GROW IN THE DIRT.
IT'S SO
GROSS!
YOUR GENERATION
IS SPOILED ROTTEN!
BOO HOO!
I'M SO SAD
ABOUT LIFE!
WHEN I WAS
A KID WE HAD
SUMMER JOBS!
AND PIZZA
TASTED LIKE
CARDBOARD!
AND WE
LIKED IT!

OKAY, I WILL STOP CRYING.
BUT WHAT AM I GOING TO EAT NOW?

CRUNCH!

GIVE ME A POTATO!
END!

"ZINE CLUB" BY PHILLIPE RICARD.

BADSTEW.NET

PLEASE KEEP WARM

TALES TO CHILL

STORY BY: MICHAEL SWEATER ART BY: BENJI NATE

MOVIE NIGHT!
MOVIE NIGHT!
MOVIE NIGHT!

MOVIE NIGHT!
MOVIE NIGHT!

YOU'RE SUPPOSED TO BE SLEEPING!
WHY ARE YOU OUT OF BED?
I SMELLED POPCORN.

PRETTY EXCITING STUFF.
CLOVER'S FIRST SCARY MOVIE!

I DUNNO IF THIS IS A GOOD IDEA...

CLOVER IS KIND OF SENSITIVE.

NAH, THIS MOVIE LOOKS PRETTY SILLY.
VAMPIRE PRESIDENT

WHAT'S THE WORST THAT COULD HAPPEN?

PRESIDENT DRACULA, YOU HAVE TRULY BROUGHT THIS DIVIDED NATION TOGETHER.

HAHA!
ITS FUNNY HOW VAMPIRES AREN'T REAL, HUH?
HA!
DO YOU WANT ME TO GET YOUR NIGHT LIGHT?

YAWN

RUSTLE

GASP

MOW!
JAMES!

WHAT ARE YOU DOING IN HERE?

I'M TOO YOUNG TO HAVE A HEART ATTACK!
PURRRR

GASP

HI CLOVER!

AHHHH!!

HEY CLOVER. WHAT'S COOKIN'?

I KNOW VAMPIRES AREN'T REAL BUT I'M STILL SCARED.
AM I GONNA BE SCARED FOR THE REST OF MY LIFE?
MAYBE.
I'M SCARED ALL THE TIME.

NEXT TIME ON "DRAGON ORBS"...
GASP
AFTER THAT CORNDOG ITS TIME FOR BED.
AND DON'T WORRY...
I MADE SURE THERE WEREN'T ANY VAMPIRE *PRESIDENTS* UNDER YOUR BED!
HAHA HAHA HAHA!!
BUT HE DIDN'T EVEN CHECK THE *CLOSET.*
AMATUER.

IT'S OKAY, FROGBOY...
I'M SCARED TOO BUT DON'T WORRY.
I'VE TAKEN EXTRA PRECAUTIONS.
CLICK
WHAT THE HECK?
PLEASE DO NOT MURDER!

PLEASE KEEP WARM IS DRAWN BY MICHAEL SWEATER IN PHILADELPHIA.

THIS BOOK WAS MADE POSSIBLE BY RACHEL DUKES, AVI THE GREAT, AND THE MAGNIFICENT BENJI NATE.

YOU CAN WITNESS MY SCIENCE AT WWW.MICHAELSWEATER.COM

MORE VITAL COMICS FROM SILVER SPROCKET

STORE.SILVERSPROCKET.NET